A Panda Grows Up

By Rita Golden Gelman • Illustrated by Mary Morgan

SCHOLASTIC INC.

New York   Toronto   London   Auckland   Sydney

ISBN 0-590-43612-0

12 11 10 9 8 7 6 5 4 3 2 1   3 4 5 6 7 8/9

Printed in the U.S.A.   08

First Scholastic printing, February 1993

For Sarah Brook Fang
and Zachary Brook Fang

— R.G.G.

GIANT PANDAS live in the mountains of central China.
The word *panda* means "bamboo eater."
In China, pandas are called *daxiong mao* (da-she-ong mao), which means "great bearcat."
Pandas grow to be 62 to 70 inches (160 to 180 centimeters) long.
Fully grown pandas usually weigh from 187 to 243 pounds (85 to 110 kilograms).

Newborn panda babies are about 6 inches (15 centimeters) long.
They live with their mothers until they are around
one and a half years old.
Then they go off on their own.

This is the story of one little panda.

It was spring.

The streams were waterfalling over the rocks.

Monkeys were skittering through the trees.

Cuckoos were calling.

A laughing thrush was sitting in the middle of a bamboo grove.

A few feet away from the bird, a giant panda
stretched her big black paws and yawned.

Then she began to climb.

She walked slowly, with her toes pointed in and
her head held low.

Now and then she stopped to rub her scent
on rocks, on stumps, on the ground.

When she reached the top of the hill, she rubbed against a tree.

Then she clawed at the moss-covered bark.

Later that day a male panda sniffed the tree.
He looked at the fresh claw marks.
And he knew that there was a female nearby
who wanted to mate.
He climbed the tree.
He barked and chirped and bleated.

That night he found the female.
He followed her all the next day and night.
Together they barked and chirped and bleated,
and in the morning they mated.
Soon after, the male left.

The female ate and slept and drank as always.
But now, inside her, a baby was growing.
Five months later she stopped eating and began making a nest.
She carried some twigs and branches into a hollow tree.
She clawed wood shavings from the rotten wood inside,
and she made a little mound.

When the baby was ready to be born,
the mother leaned against the tree.
Soon, a tiny baby came out of her.
She lifted him from between her legs with her mouth.
He was pink, and his ears were flat against his body.
His eyes were tightly closed.
She put him in her big furry paw and licked his back,
his face, his belly, his bottom.
Then she held him to her breast, and he drank.

The baby spent most of his time in his mother's paw.

When he was hungry, he squawked.

When he was dangling upside down, he squawked.

When she squeezed him too hard, or not hard enough, he squawked.

His mother heard his complaints and was always there to take care of him.

Wherever she went, she carried him in her paw
or in her mouth.
The baby panda drank a lot of milk and grew quickly.

One day, when he was two months old,
his mother put him down on a soft mound of wood chips.
The little panda's eyes were only half opened,
but he knew that his mother had left him.
He squealed.

The baby never saw the leopard.
But the two squirrels did.
They raced up a tree, chittering.
A monkey screeched out a warning.
Other monkeys scrambled to the tops of the trees.
The leopard came closer.

The mother panda heard the monkey-warning.
She ran to her baby, growling and roaring
and chattering her teeth.
The leopard ran away.
For a long time after that, the mother held the baby in her arms.

Later that day the mother and baby moved to a nearby cave.

Over the next few months the baby grew quickly.
Soon he was able to play.
He wrestled with his mother's leg.
He climbed on her back and somersaulted off.
He slid down snowbanks.
He climbed trees.

Winter was cold and snowy.
But the little panda was never cold.
His rough outside fur was wet from the snow,
but his soft oily underfur kept him warm and dry.

By his first spring the little panda had grown enough
to eat bamboo shoots.
He learned from his mother how to peel the outside
and crunch the juicy inside of the shoots.
To hold the bamboo, he used his sixth finger like a thumb.

For three months he and his mother ate bamboo shoots and young stems.
In just one day they ate more than 3,000 bamboo stems.
Much of what the young panda ate was too tough for him to digest.
More than half of what he ate came back out again in droppings.

For a whole year the panda and his mother did
the same thing every day.
In the spring, in the summer, in the fall, in the winter,
they walked and ate and walked and ate and slept.
They drank as well.
Sometimes they drank so much that they couldn't even walk.
They just collapsed near the stream.

When the little panda was about one and a half years old,
he was big enough to be on his own.
One day he walked away from his mother, perhaps never to see her again.

For days and months he walked and ate and walked and ate.
Sometimes he heard noises that frightened him,
and he hid in a clump of bamboo.
One time he just barely escaped from a leopard
by swimming across a stream.

One bright winter night the little panda was walking.
His feet crunched the frozen grasses and leaves.
Suddenly he heard a pack of wild dogs.
He scampered up a tree, digging his sharp claws
into the mossy bark.
The dogs heard the panda from a distance.
They smelled the panda from up close.
But they couldn't get to him.
He was safe in the tree.

When the little panda was nearly five years old,
something terrible happened.
The bamboo flowered.
It was spring.
Everything was dripping from the rain.
The ground was spongy and wet.
The little panda didn't know it, but when bamboo flowers
in the spring, it dies in the autumn and there is no food.
(It doesn't happen very often — maybe once
every forty or sixty or one hundred years.)

When the bamboo died, there was nothing to eat.
The panda walked and sniffed and searched.
He walked and walked and walked.
He did not know there was bamboo
on the other side of the mountain.
It was too far away.

Day by day he grew weaker.
Soon he was too weak to climb.
And then he was almost too weak to walk.
When he lay down, he could barely get up again.

Then, late one night, he smelled food.
He followed the smell down the hill,
through an open patch of land,
and right into a cage.
The door slammed shut.

He pushed with his head.
He shoved with his shoulder.
He gnawed with his teeth.
But there was no way he could get out.

In the morning, people came.
They gave the panda medicine that put him to sleep.
Then they carried him to their camp.
They weighed him and measured him.
They put a white radio collar around his neck.
And they gave him all the food he wanted.

The people were scientists who were studying pandas.
They were also trying to save pandas from starvation.

For three weeks, the panda wandered around the research camp.
When he was strong again, the scientists took him
to the other side of the mountain where there was plenty of bamboo.

The panda was five years old.
He walked and ate and walked and ate and slept.
Every once in a while he ate something new: a mushroom
or a root or a piece of fruit.
Sometimes he attacked a beehive and ate some honey.
Occasionally he caught a rat and ate it, skin and bones and all.
But most of the time he ate bamboo . . . the shoots, the stems,
and the leaves.

Finally it was spring again.
Water from the melting snow was crashing down the mountains.
Plants were bursting into flower.
Birds were filling the thickets with their songs.

One day the panda sniffed a rock and a stump and a tree.
He saw freshly clawed marks in the bark of the tree.
And he knew there was a female nearby who was ready to mate.
He climbed the tree.
He barked and chirped and bleated.
That night he found the female.

Giant pandas are an endangered species.
In the past, they were hunted for their skins,
and their bamboo forests were cut down
to make room for people.
Also, many pandas died of starvation
when the bamboo flowered.
Today there are only about 1,000 pandas
in the whole world.
The government of China
and people all over the world
are trying to save the giant panda
from becoming extinct.